ICE AGE
ESCAPE

Sue Graves

Rising Stars UK Ltd.
7 Hatchers Mews, Bermondsey Street, London SE1 3GS
www.risingstars-uk.com

nasen

NASEN House, 4/5 Amber Business Village, Amber Close,
Amington, Tamworth, Staffordshire B77 4RP

Published 2012

Author: Sue Graves
Series editor: Sasha Morton
Text and logo design: pentacor**big**
Typesetting: Geoff Rayner, Bag of Badgers
Cover design: Lon Chan
Project Manager: Sasha Morton Creative Project Management
Editorial: Deborah Kespert
Artwork: Colour: Lon Chan / B&W: Paul Loudon

British Library Cataloguing in Publication Data.
A CIP record for this book is available from the British Library.

ISBN: 978-0-85769-608-3

Printed by Craftprint International, Singapore

It was Saturday morning and Tom, Sima and Kojo were hanging out together. They all worked at Dangerous Games, a computer games company. Sima designed the games. Kojo programmed them and Tom tested them to see if they were satisfying to play. They all loved their jobs and they were best mates, too.

Later that day, Tom, Sima and Kojo went to the dinosaur exhibition at the City Museum. Some of the dinosaurs were massive, but some weren't so big. Some of the dinosaurs looked really scary, but some didn't look very scary at all.

"I wonder if dinosaurs lived all over the world," said Kojo.

"No idea," said Sima. "I'm just glad I wasn't alive at the time. Coming face-to-face with a dinosaur is not my idea of fun at all."

Just then, one of the curators walked by.

"Nasty looking beast, that one," he said, nodding at the large dinosaur skeleton. "I bet you wouldn't like to meet him on a dark night! Look at those enormous teeth. They would easily take a huge chunk out of you."

Sima took a closer look. Each tooth was bright yellow and longer than her hand. The teeth were very sharp, too. She shivered. "It must have been a terrifying creature," she said.

"Did dinosaurs live all over the world?" asked Kojo.

"That's an interesting question," said the curator. For a long time we thought they only lived in some parts of the world, but now we are not so sure. There's been a recent discovery in the Antarctic of a dinosaur bone. Our scientists are amazed that dinosaurs actually lived so far south and in such a cold place."

"That *is* amazing," agreed Tom.

The curator looked at his watch. "Well, I must get back to work. We close in half an hour." He grinned as he walked off. "Don't get locked in with the dinosaurs."

When the curator had gone, Tom rubbed his hands together excitedly.

"What's up with you?" said Sima.

"That man has just given me a brilliant idea for our new game."

Kojo looked puzzled. "Did I miss something?"

"You certainly did," said Tom. "Don't you think it's amazing that dinosaurs lived in the Antarctic?"

"Yeah, I suppose so," said Kojo.

"Well, why don't we create a new game about dinosaurs in the Antarctic? It would be a brilliant setting and I bet you could make it really exciting, Sima."

"Sounds promising," agreed Sima, smiling. "First thing on Monday morning, I'll get to work on the designs. Meanwhile, how about getting something to eat? I'm starving."

CHAPTER 2

On Monday morning, Sima began work on the designs for the new game. She told the boys all about it.

"The players have to find dinosaur bones and build the creature before the game time runs out," she explained. "And to make things more interesting, they have to cope with Antarctic conditions, so there will be plenty of ice, blizzards and really freezing temperatures."

"Sounds OK ... I think," said Tom, doubtfully.

"What's up?" asked Kojo." Don't you like Sima's ideas?"

"I do," said Tom, "but I'm wondering if we could make it a bit more exciting. How about if we add creatures that make it more difficult for the players to build the dinosaur?"

"What sort of creatures?" asked Sima.

Tom grabbed a piece of paper and picked up his pen. He began to draw some large, angry-looking birds. The birds had long talons and huge beaks that curved into sharp spikes. "How about including these birds? We could call them ice eagles," he said.

"They look gruesome," said Sima.

"They look horrendous," said Kojo.

"So you like them?" asked Tom.

"Yes, I do. They're great," said Kojo.

"I'm just a bit worried," said Sima, "that by adding those birds, we might make the game too dangerous. Also they might be too difficult for Kojo to program."

"No, I think I can make it work," said Kojo.

"Excellent," said Tom.

"Oh dear," sighed Sima.

By Wednesday, the designs were finished and Kojo had programmed the game.

"I'm afraid I couldn't include the ice eagles, after all," he said. "It would make the game too expensive to produce. It has to be the same price as all our other ones."

"Boring!" said Tom and he winked at Sima.

"I think we ought to test the game for real," said Sima.

"I was hoping you'd say that," said Tom. "But you're not usually keen."

"I know," said Sima. "But I'm a bit worried about this game. I want the play value to be good but I don't want it to be too tricky either."

Tom pulled out a scarf and a woolly hat from his desk drawer. "Ready for testing!" he said.

Sima laughed. "I don't think so, not dressed like that." She pulled out a bag from under her desk. "I've hired us some proper Antarctic clothing and some special equipment, too. Tonight when we test the game, we must all be properly equipped."

When everyone else at Dangerous Games had gone home, Tom, Sima and Kojo put on the layers of special Antarctic clothing Sima had hired. Then they put the equipment they needed into a large bag. Finally, Kojo loaded the game onto his computer.

"Don't forget the rules," he said. "We all ..."

"... touch the screen at the same time to enter the game," interrupted Tom.

"Yes, yes," said Kojo. "And the game ..."

"... is only over when we hear the words 'Game over'," interrupted Sima as they all laughed.

"So let's do it!" said Kojo.

They all touched the screen together. A bright light flashed and they shut their eyes tightly.

CHAPTER 3

The bright light faded and Tom, Sima and Kojo opened their eyes. They were standing on thick ice in the Antarctic and it was really, really cold. A blizzard was raging and it was hard to see anything at all.

WHOA! IT'S FREEZING.

THE ANTARCTIC IS KNOWN TO BE FREEZING, TOM!

"I think I'd like to get through this game as quickly as possible, before we all freeze to death. Let's spread out and see if we can find some of the dinosaur bones," suggested Sima.

59:00

Kojo handed each of them an ice pick from a bag on the ground and they set to work. But the ice was so hard it was impossible to hack into. After ten minutes, Kojo and Sima had found nothing and Tom had only found one dinosaur leg bone. He threw down his ice pick angrily.

THIS GAME'S RUBBISH, SIMA. IT TAKES TOO LONG TO FIND ANYTHING.

42:00

Sima was upset. "This is why I wanted to test it for real," she said. "I had a horrible feeling it might not work out properly. I'm so sorry."

21

Kojo looked at his watch. "I can't see any point in continuing with this game," he said. "Shall I try and abort it?"

I DON'T THINK WE SHOULD GIVE UP SO EASILY.

"I agree with Kojo," said Tom. "There's no point in continuing with the game at all." He tossed the leg bone up in the air. The bone spun round and round. Then it started to spin faster and faster. Suddenly it shot downwards and sliced into the ice like a dagger. The ice shattered around it like broken glass.

"How weird is that?" said Tom. He strode over to check it out. The bone was sticking straight up out of the ice and it was quivering.

Sima and Kojo joined Tom. Kojo nudged the bone with his foot, then he stared hard at the ground. "What's that under the ice?" he said. He knelt down. "There's a strange shape under here. Look."

Tom and Sima knelt down beside him. The shape under the ice was long and dark. "Perhaps it's buried treasure," suggested Sima.

"Don't be crazy," said Tom. "Who would want to bury treasure deep under the ice in the middle of the Antarctic?"

LET'S SEE IF WE CAN UNEARTH IT.

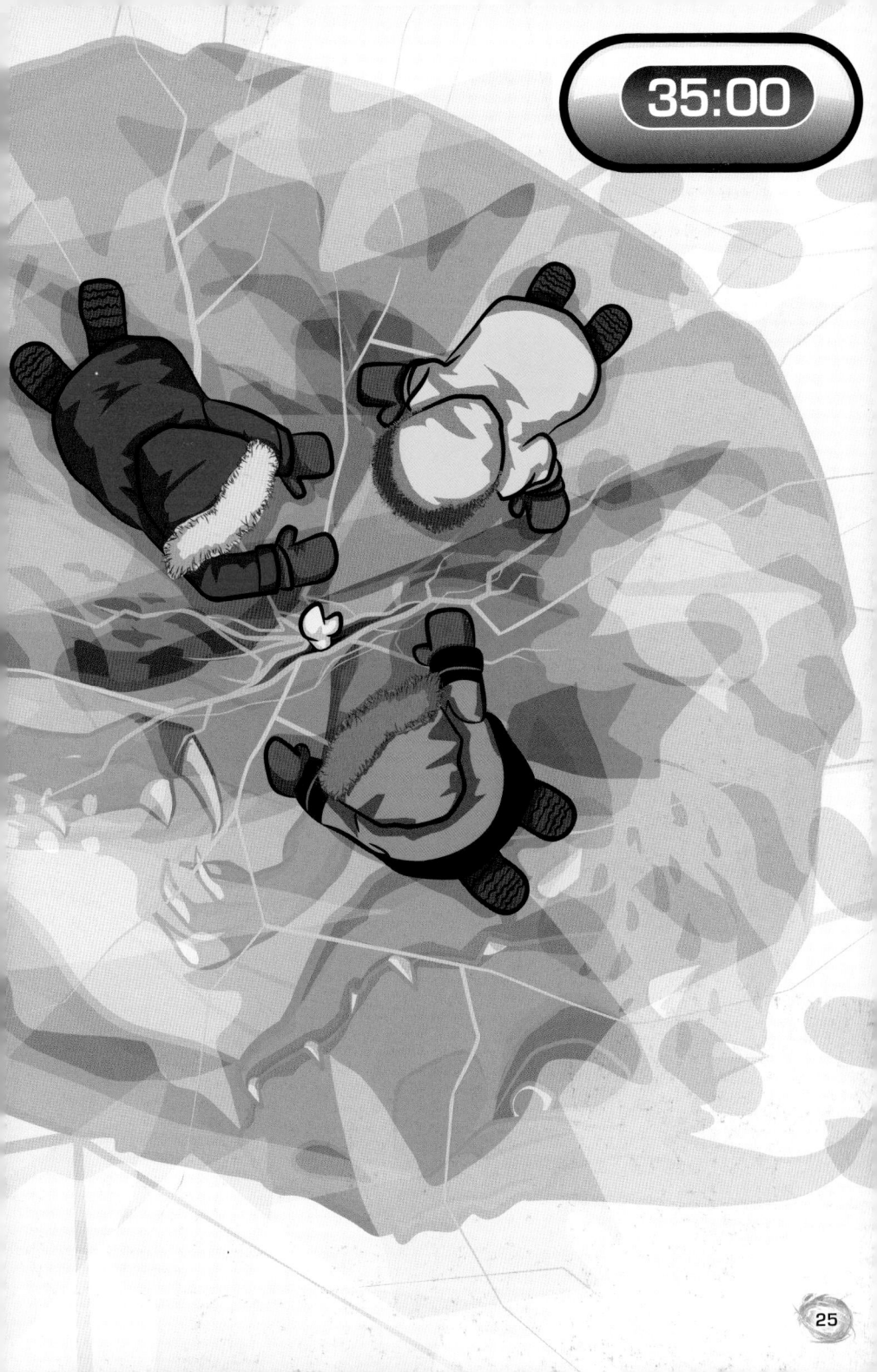

Kojo fetched the ice picks and they all set to work. After a while, Kojo sat back on his heels. His face was as white as a sheet.

WHAT'S UP?

"I think we have found the remains of a whole dinosaur!" Kojo exclaimed.

"Excellent!" said Tom and he struck the ice harder with his ice pick.

Kojo slowly stood up and started backing away, "It's not excellent at all," he whispered. "I think I saw its eye move."

"No way!" said Tom. "I haven't noticed any movement at all. Anyway, it can only be a dinosaur skeleton. It can't be alive or anything."

"Yes," said Sima. "The aim of the game was to build a dinosaur bone-by-bone. I must have messed up the designs a little and instead we've discovered a complete skeleton. Never mind, at least we can complete the game now."

"I'm telling you, I saw it move," insisted Kojo.

CHAPTER 4

Tom and Sima moved away but as they did so the ice erupted with an enormous crack and a huge dinosaur rose from the ground. Its body was black and it had a large scaly head and long, yellow teeth. The dinosaur rose up on its back legs and, opening its mouth wide, let out a deafening roar.

RUN FOR IT!

Everyone ran as fast as they could, but the dinosaur was close behind … and it was catching up fast.

Suddenly, Sima spotted a large ridge of ice in front of them. There was a small gap at the bottom of the ridge. "Follow me," she shouted.

They ran to the gap in the ridge and squeezed inside. The dinosaur roared with rage and tried to force its head inside the narrow crack. Its breath smelt sour and stale.

DO SOMETHING!

WE DON'T HAVE TIME TO DO ANYTHING!

"We can't leave the game with this creature still alive!" cried Sima. "It could get back into the real world."

"Ice eagles!" shouted Tom. "We must activate the ice eagles."

"I told you I couldn't program them into the game," said Kojo.

"I know you did," said Tom. "But I thought I would have a go at creating them myself. Hopefully I can control them with this …"

Tom reached inside his pocket and took out a small console.

"Where did you get that from?" asked Kojo.

"It's from one of our old games," said Tom. "I found it at the back of the store cupboard in the office. I thought I would fiddle around and see what I could come up with. I had a feeling you'd say that including the ice eagles would make the game too expensive. So I thought I'd create them myself."

Kojo's mouth dropped open. "How could you?" he said. "That's against all the rules at Dangerous Games. Mr Wilson would go mad if he found out."

"This is no time to worry about rules," retorted Sima. She turned to Tom. "Let's just hope the ice eagles can save us and the real world from this dinosaur."

ACTIVATE THE ICE EAGLES, TOM!

Tom activated the console. Suddenly, they could hear a loud whooshing noise. The dinosaur gave a loud roar and moved away from the gap.

"Sounds promising," said Tom and he carefully peered out of the gap to see what was happening. He looked up and saw that the sky was black with large, angry-looking birds. They had long talons and huge beaks that curved into sharp spikes and they were circling the dinosaur.

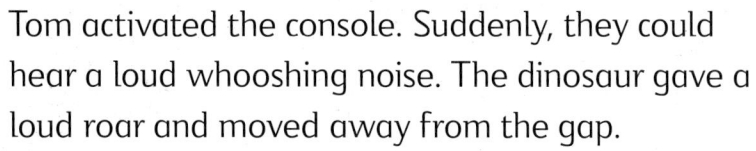

THIS IS GOING TO BE GOOD!

Tom directed the birds closer to the dinosaur and pressed a button. The ice eagles swooped down and, screeching loudly, attacked the dinosaur. The air was filled with the animal's roars as it tried to defend itself, but the birds kept attacking until the dinosaur lay dead on the ice. Its blood ran in a thick red line along the ice and froze solid.

Tom pressed another button on the console and they watched as the ice eagles vaporised into a black swirling mist. Just then, a bright light flashed. They closed their eyes tightly.

CHAPTER 5

The bright light faded. Tom, Sima and Kojo were back in the office. They were all shivering and shocked, and they sat quietly for a few minutes before anyone spoke.

"We can't possibly market that game," said Sima. "It's horrifying."

"I agree," said Kojo, pulling off his heavy, fur-lined jacket and throwing it over a chair. Even though they were still wearing layers of protective clothing, they were all wet and shivering.

"Don't be too hasty," said Tom. "It was really exciting and unpredictable. Gamers would love it, especially if we include the ice eagles. I don't think they'd mind paying a little extra for a feature like that."

Sima and Kojo looked unconvinced and Tom laughed. "You two are so unadventurous!" he chuckled.

Tom looked at his watch. "Come on, let's go to Frankie's Café. It's open late tonight. We can chill out there and I'll try and convince you that the game is a good one." Then he grinned. "And as a special treat I'll buy both of you some very large ice-creams!"

GLOSSARY OF TERMS

abort end something before it is completed

Antarctic a very cold region in the southern-most part of the world

blizzard(s) a storm of strong winds and snow

console a board with switches that is used to control a machine or electronic equipment

curator someone whose job it is to look after objects in a museum

equipment tools or machines that do a particular job or activity

horrendous extremely horrible or bad

ice pick a tool that has a sharp point for breaking ice

nudge(d) to use part of your body to push something

remains dead body

talon(s) sharp claws

temperature(s) the measurement that tells us how hot or cold something is

vaporised changed into a vapour

Quiz

1   What exhibits were at the museum?

2   Where did the curator say that dinosaur bones had recently been found?

3   What sorts of creatures did Tom want to add to the game?

4   Why did he want to add them?

5   What part of the dinosaur, buried under the ice, did Kojo say moved?

6   Where did Sima, Kojo and Tom hide from the dinosaur?

7   What did Tom use to activate the birds?

8   What did the birds do to the dinosaur?

9   What happened to the birds afterwards?

10 What did Tom say he was going to treat Kojo and Sima to?

ABOUT THE AUTHOR

Sue Graves has taught for thirty years in Cheshire schools. She has been writing for more than ten years and has written well over a hundred books for children and young adults.

"Nearly everyone loves computer games. They are popular with all age groups — especially young adults. But I've often thought it would be amazing to play a computer game for real. To be in on the action would be the best experience ever! That's why I wrote these stories. I hope you enjoy reading them as much as I've enjoyed writing them for you."

ANSWERS TO QUIZ

1 Dinosaur exhibits

2 The Antarctic

3 Ice eagles

4 To make the game more exciting and more difficult

5 Its eyes

6 A gap in a ridge

7 A console

8 They killed it

9 They vaporised

10 Large ice-creams